The

Case #1:

The Mystery of
the Moody Ghost

KEEP OUT!

By Robin Dunne and James Kee

Based on the television movie screenplay by
Robin Dunne and James Kee

PSS!
PRICE STERN SLOAN

PRICE STERN SLOAN
Published by the Penguin Group
Penguin Group (USA) Inc., 375 Hudson Street, New York,
New York 10014, USA
Penguin Group (Canada), 90 Eglinton Avenue East, Suite 700,
Toronto, Ontario M4P 2Y3, Canada
(a division of Pearson Penguin Canada Inc.)
Penguin Books Ltd., 80 Strand, London WC2R 0RL, England
Penguin Group Ireland, 25 St. Stephen's Green, Dublin 2, Ireland
(a division of Penguin Books Ltd.)
Penguin Group (Australia), 250 Camberwell Road, Camberwell,
Victoria 3124, Australia (a division of Pearson Australia Group Pty. Ltd.)
Penguin Books India Pvt. Ltd., 11 Community Centre, Panchsheel Park,
New Delhi—110 017, India
Penguin Group (NZ), 67 Apollo Drive, Rosedale, North Shore 0632,
New Zealand (a division of Pearson New Zealand Ltd.)
Penguin Books (South Africa) (Pty.) Ltd., 24 Sturdee Avenue,
Rosebank, Johannesburg 2196, South Africa

Penguin Books Ltd., Registered Offices:
80 Strand, London WC2R 0RL, England

The scanning, uploading, and distribution of this book via the Internet
or via any other means without the permission of the publisher is illegal
and punishable by law. Please purchase only authorized electronic editions and
do not participate in or encourage electronic piracy of copyrighted materials.
Your support of the authors' rights is appreciated.

© 2008 Roxy Hunter, LLC. Roxy Hunter is a trademark of Roxy Hunter, LLC.
Used under license by Penguin Young Readers Group. All rights reserved.
Published by Price Stern Sloan, a division of Penguin Young Readers Group,
345 Hudson Street, New York, New York 10014. PSS! is a registered trademark
of Penguin Group (USA) Inc. Printed in the U.S.A.

Library of Congress Control Number: 2006101208

ISBN 978-0-8431-2664-8   10 9 8 7 6 5 4 3 2 1

WARNING

The contents of this journal are the super-top-secret possession of Roxanne Hunter. Also known as Roxy. Please do not read any farther. Stop right there. You're still reading. All right, if you're suffering from curiosification*, then read the next part. If this journal is found, please return by any means necessary (carrier pigeon, helicopter, tangerine-colored zeppelin) to:

Roxy Hunter, Super-Sleuth,
Moody Mansion, Serenity Falls, Earth, Universe.
Thank you.

A Note from Max

Hello. In the interest of clarity, I've taken the liberty of including "Max Facts." These are (hopefully) the correct interpretations of Roxy's unique words, followed by the definitions.

*curiosification:
curiosity: a strong desire
to learn or know something

New York:
A Leaving Poem

Good-bye, my home and dear friend.
I know not when we'll meet again.
So long, Central Park. Bye-bye, MoMA*,
I'm off to live in a culture coma.
I trade my <u>Big Apple</u> heart and the city lights
For barnyards filled with ticks and mites.
So, to my city, I say "good-bye."
I can write no more—it's time to cry.

Parting is such sweet sorrow.

I ♥ NYC

Dear faithful journal:

It is the last night ever in my bedroom. My entire earthly belongings lie in boxes scattered about.

As is my heart.

My mom got a job at a bank—great! Except that it's in the wilds of Country Pumpkin, USA.

Population: **BORING!**

The bank has arranged a house for us to move into. I sincerely hope it has running water. And electricity. And no cattle in the kitchen. Good-bye, Broadway. Good-bye, Times Square. Good-bye, Met*.

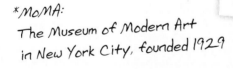

Max Facts

*MoMA:
The Museum of Modern Art
in New York City, founded 1929

*Met:
The Metropolitan Opera,
founded 1883

This is me, Max (my fiancé & family friend), and my formerly lovely mother. This is my little family in happier times. So innocent. So trusting.

This is me now...

I call this picture "THE UNHAPPIEST VOYAGE" or "CAR RIDE OF THE DOOMED."

Dear faithful journal:

Hey, I just saw the first butterfly of spring go by. Why are they called "butterflies"? They don't look like flies. And, as far as I know, they don't have the slightest interest in butter. Or in margarine, for that matter. To me they look like peacocks. Miniature, fluttering, flowery peacocks. I hereby change their name. Those who were formerly butterflies shall now go by the name of miniflutterflowerpocks.

THE HOUSE IS AMAZING!

Dear faithful journal:

I love it! It's sooo huge! It's like a castle! I feel
like Lady Roxanne Hunter of Hamalot*! I plan on
hostessing an eggnoggural ball*, complete with horse
chariots and fireworks and jugglers and those funny
men on walking sticks. And mimes. Wait. No mimes.
Mimes are... odd. But the best part is that a
couple local kids stopped by (they get a ten on
the doofus scale). And guess what they told us...
THE HOUSE IS HAUNTED! The house has been
abandoned for years and years, but just last week
STRANGE LIGHTS were seen in the attic window!
THIS DEMANDS AN INVESTIGATION!

DUCK CHIN CHU*

The Ancient Oriental Art of BRAIN KICKING*.
As taught to Max by the Wu Tan Masters of Indonesia. This ancient art can be used whenever you are up against neighborhood bullies. (As Max could have today when he was defending my honor.)

*Hamalot:
Camelot: the legendary court of King Arthur

*eggnoggural ball:
inaugural ball: a celebration for the president at the beginning of a term of office

*I can find no reference to Oriental Brain Kicking. Duck Chin Chu is apparently a soup.

Max Facts

Midnight.

Cannot sleep.

Why, you ask?

AAAAAAHHHH!!!!

The house IS haunted!

Do you have any idea what sleep deprimation* does to someone my age?

We are sleeping in the living room because the furnace is broken. And there are thunking, clunking noises coming from upstairs. And as Mom and Max sleep peacefully, I lie here in cold terror—trembling. I don't know if this will be my last entry, oh faithful journal.

GHOSTS

What I know:

1. They don't wear sheets. Chains to carry around are an optional accessory.
2. They are clumsy and make noise. Like a pony on roller skates.
3. You may be frightened of ghosts, but remember: They are MORE FRIGHTENED OF YOU!
4. They make your breath so winter fresh, you can see it.
5. They are trapped in an endless cycle of despair. Very similar to when you have a bad substitute teacher who doesn't understand you.
   Yes, I mean YOU, Mr. Lawson!

Max Fact

*sleep deprimation:
sleep deprivation: lacking sufficient sleep

How to start a healthy morning in a Haunted House (or any house, really):

SMOOTHIE RECIPES

A smoothie is a drink you make in a blender. Smoothies are healthy and packed with vital nourishments, but better than all that—they're YUMMILICIOUS*!

Try these, then make up your own.

THE STRAWBLUKI

2 cups SOY MILK, 1 BANANA (for best results, peel banana), 10 BLUEBERRIES, 1 KIWI (peeled—even though they have fur, it is not cruelty to peel them), 5 STRAWBERRIES

THE CARIBINNAMON

2 cups SOY MILK, 1 BANANA, 1 handful CAROB CHIPS, 3 dashes of CINNAMON (or a "dollop" as is the technational* term). Blend them up, and slurp them down.

To all nonbelievers
(Max and Mom):
I TOLD YOU SO!

The haunted plaster

Oh, faithful journal,
while Mom was talking
to the estate lawyer,
REBECCA, who's here
doing repairs on the house all week (and apparently
babysitting me as well—as if I need that!), a chunk of
plaster spontageously* fell from the ceiling. I declare
this house officially haunted! I hereby commence the
investigation of the ghost in the attic.

BY THE WAY—
an estate is something
that happens after you die.
The owner of this home,
Estelle Moody, died, and
now the estate owns her
property. Weird.

*yummilicious: yummy + delicious

*technational:
   technical: based on strict
   interpretation

*spontageously:
   spontaneously: occurring without
   apparent external cause

Max Facts

HOW TO DO AN INVESTIGATION

1. Look for **CLUES**. Clues, clues, and more clues. There can be many different kinds: fingerprints, footprints, or an unusual shade of lipstick on a glass.
2. Suspect **EVERYONE**. I mean EVERYONE is a suspect.
3. Process of **ELIMITATION***. By elimitating* people, they are no longer suspects. Just make sure they don't leave town.
4. Always remember: The **TRUTH** wants to be **DISCOVERED!**

Max Facts

*process of elimitation:
process of elimination:
solving problems by removing variables one after another

*elimitating:
eliminating:
removing variables one at a time

Today's Discovery

Max and I went outside to investigate the yard—
and guess what we found? Go on, guess! Give up?
We found a window open in the attic. So Max
and I went upstairs where we found a really cool
secret door that we think leads up to the attic—
because otherwise, the only way to get there would
be by helicopter.

This is the door. The door is very small.
Apparently hobbits used to live here.
Unfortunately, they padlocked the door.
Mom came home and interrupted our investigation.
I am reluctant to inform
her of our findings.
Parents just get
frightened when presented
with portholes of the
unknown. Operation Attic
Door commences tomorrow.

Midnight Entry

I can hear the ghost's footsteps clunking in the attic yet again. I went to check on Max to see if he could hear it as well. He could. The poor dear, his scientific brain does not compute the obleakitosity* of the supernatural world of the beyond like mine does. I look forward to meeting our phantom friend tomorrow.

Max Fact

*obleakitosity:
I have no idea

In any operation or investigation, code names are very important to congeal* your identity in top-secretosity*. Security is of super-supreme importance.

CODE NAMES:

Mom = Eagle One
Me = Winnie the Pooh (team leader)

Max = Piglet

TARGET OF MISSION:

1. To get lock off hobbit door
2. To get into attic
3. To find CLUES as to who-abouts* of ghost
4. To trap said ghost

Let's rumble.

Pooh out.

Max Facts

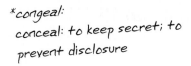

*congeal:
conceal: to keep secret; to prevent disclosure

*top-secretosity:
the condition of being top-secret

*who-abouts:
whereabouts: the place where a person or object is

Accessorizing for an Investigation

What would Sherlock Holmes be without his famous hat? What would Humpty Boogert* be without his trench coat? What would Roxy Hunter be without her earrings?

Accessorizing for an investigation is a VERY serious thing. It is of up most* importance! You are making a statement. That statement is: "I am a detective. You are not."

Max Facts

*Humpty Boogert:
Humphrey Bogart (1899–1957):
Hollywood film star and icon; best known for <u>Casablanca</u> and <u>The Maltese Falcon</u>

*up most:
utmost: to the greatest degree

I am brilliant!

We finally got into the attic. Max thinks the strange noises were made by raccoons because the window was open. But I found a box with old papers and things.

Then I found…
Her ENGAGEMENT RING!
Estelle Moody is the ghost!
And she is trying to reunificate* with her lost love T. C.!

Note: find out who T. C. is. He is the hole in the donut of this mystery.

This is Estelle Moody. She used to own this house.

Max Facts

The prescription* on the ring says: "E. M. Forever T. C."

*reunificate: to reunite

*prescription:
inscription: something that is written, usually a dedication, on a hard material

Journal, obviously you know
it is time for...

HOW TO BUILD A GHOST TRAP

1. Find something to trap the ghost with—a blanket will work nicely.

2. Hang the blanket from the ceiling using a rope or yarn.

3. Attach the rope or yarn to the window. That way, when the window goes up, the rope will lower the blanket down over your ghost—
TRAPPING IT!

VOILÀ! ONE TRAPPED GHOST!

I must contact the spirit of Estelle Moody in order to find out who T. C. is, and relieve her suffering on this mortal broil*.

I will conduct a séance tonight. One of the local yokels, Seth (soooo lame), has challenged my ability to contact the other world.

He will regret the day he ever doubted...

Madame Roxanne Dupuis d'Hunterre—

the spiritualist from beyond!

Now to find an outfit!

Max Fact

*mortal broil:
mortal coil: from <u>Hamlet</u>
by William Shakespeare;
meaning the "mortal world"

MADAME ROXANNE DUPUIS D'HUNTERRE'S GUIDE TO QUALITY CONTACTING THE SPIRITS OF THE LONG DEPARTURED*

1. Dress the part. No one takes a badly dressed spirit contactor seriously.
2. Candlelight. Duh.
3. A personal affectation* of the departured.
4. Be spooky.
5. Improvise the rest.

This is the look you are going for.

Max Facts

*departured:
departed: someone who is no longer alive

*affectation:
effect: something that belongs or belonged to somebody

ANOTHER CASE CLOSED BY ROXY HUNTER— SUPER-SLEUTH!

Now, the trick is to let him stay without Mom finding out.

During my brilliant séance, just when I actually contacted the world beyond, my ghost trap in the attic was tripped! It worked! But when Max and I got up there, we discovered we hadn't caught a ghost, we had caught a...

RAMMA!

Apparently a Ramma is a sleep-deprimated* medical student studying for exams who also has no money so he must live in attics of formerly abandoned houses. (Boy, Doctor School must be really expensive!!)
The poor thing! He's such a sweet man.
Just look at him!

Max Fact
↘

*sleep-deprimated: sleep-deprived

23

oh, faithful journal,

I know what you're thinking: Why aren't you telling Mom about the Ramma in the attic? That's really pushing it. Okay, hear me out...

Mothers are loving, gentle, kind creatures—when it comes to their own children, or the children of friends (Max). Everyone else is a bad influence or a dreaded threat. I understand this. It is the way of the world. However, come on! You saw the picture! I know it in my bones—Ramma is a kind soul! IN MY BONES!

Ramma Creepy Meter Reading: ZERO!!
Now get off my back, will ya?

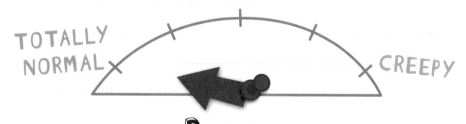

TOTALLY NORMAL — CREEPY

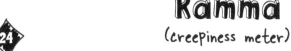

Ramma
(creepiness meter)

MAX'S PARENTS

Sometimes my dear Max is so quiet. And at those times, I think I know why. I suspect he is worrying about his parents. They are always away. It's not because they don't like him. Far from it, they love him. Everyone with a brain in their head loves Max. That is why he is my **FIANCÉ.**

But his parents are ARCHAEOLOGISTS and work in countries that I have a hard time pronouncing. (Honestly, MOST people find it hard to pronounce them.)

An archaeologist is someone who excavacuates* old buildings from long-dead civilizations. That means they dig in the dirt for things that a thousand KAJILLION years ago no one cared about— like a bit of a toothbrush, or a piece of a honey jar.

Max Fact

*excavacuates:
excavates: removes earth carefully and systematically from an area in order to find buried remains

YOU WON'T BELIEVE WHAT JUST HAPPENED!

It is the middle of the night. I've just woken up...
and there was a HAWK in my room! A real live
hawk! Just like on TV! It was perched on the dresser!

Then it picked up Estelle's ring and
FLEW OUT THE WINDOW! Don't you see?
The ghost wants the ring back!
The Case of the Noise in the Attic may be closed
(that's Ramma—shhh!). But *the Case of the
Ghost of the Ring* is open—and I'm on it!

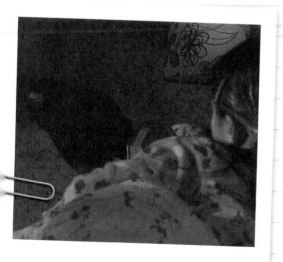

THIS PLACE
IS SO
SUPERCOOL!

This is an actual HAWK'S FEATHER from
the hawk that was in my room.
It is more than evidence. It is inspiration.

HAWK FEATHER
A POEM

Oh, noble bird that soars above
So high, so free, and so grand,
You left this feather in my room.
I really hope you don't need it to land.

Big Day

This morning I was coming down for breakfast when outside the window I saw the HAWK from last night.

The hawk wanted me to follow it—so I did! It led me to a creepy graveyard. It was sitting on a little house. (Who would live in a graveyard? Eww.) Then the hawk showed me a gravestone. And you won't believe what was on it... ESTELLE'S RING!

And if that wasn't spooktacular* enough... the grave belonged to Theodore Caruthers! T. C.! I found T. C.! This demands further investigation.

Max Fact

*spooktacular: spooky + spectacular

THIS JUST GETS BETTERER* & BETTERER

So I went into town to do some research in the library. Yes, I know I wasn't supposed to leave

the property, but us detectives are natural-born rule benders. It goes with the job. And do you know what I discovered when I got to town...?

SCANDAL!!

Mom was holding hands with some man! Can you believe it?! We've only been here a few days! If it wasn't for the demands of my investigation, I would certainly be looking into this!

Max Fact

*betterer: even better than better

BIG DAY—
THE MIDDLE

My world reeling,
I stumbled bravely to
the library.
There I met <u>Mr. Tibers</u>,
the peculiar librarian.
He seems a funny
old sort.

I have a feeling he will
be a very useful ally.
I went to work. After
hours of searching,
I found this!

The poor man.
Cut short in the
prime of his life.
War is such a waste.

War is an odd thing. Really strange. It's something grown-ups do that puzzles me. The more I think about it, the more I think things should not be decided by war. It separates people, so it is therefore the archenemy of love. I think if something is to be decided in the world, it should be decided by a checkers tournament. A huge one with a giant checkerboard and pieces the size of pizzas. In checkers, even if you lose, you don't mind. And as far as I know, no one ever died in a checkers tournament. It just doesn't make sense. We're all kind of the same. Maybe because we speak different languages we find it hard to commuticate*.
So therefore I propose that we all learn sign language! That might make it easier.

Max Fact

*commuticate:
communicate: to share information, news, and/or ideas

BIG DAY—THE REALLY BAD PART

When I got home from the library, doom awaited me.
Mom called me "Roxanne." This is a sign that I'm
REALLY in trouble.

Mom discovered Ramma. Boy, was she unseasonably* mad.
But on top of it, in the kitchen with her was the man
from the restaurant—the dreaded hand-holder, Jon (if
that's even his real name). In her misconstroodled* rage,
Mom sent me to my room. Perhaps this house is no
longer big enough for ALL OF US!
Well, if that's how it must be, I have packed my bag
and shall be gone by morning—oh, wait. That's Mom
at the door.

P.S. Mom just left. She presented a convincing
case. I guess I'll stay. Darn. I just can't help
but love that Mom of mine.

*unseasonably:
unreasonably: not guided
by judgment

*misconstroodled:
misguided? misconceived?
misconstrued? I don't know.
I really don't.

Max Facts

I miss Dad.

I thought a lot about him today. Sometimes it feels like it was a long time ago. Sometimes it feels like it was yesterday. I call these my "heavy heart days." I remember how he used to read me these books on Peruvian jungle people. They were kind of boring, so I'd fall asleep cuddled up with him. I remember the feel of his favorite flannel shirt against my face. The one that Mom was always bugging him to throw out. I always felt so safe lying against it. I would give anything to fall asleep against that flannel shirt again.

WARNING: When you are in the jungles of Peru and meet a snake, run the other way.

GOTCHA!!

Interesting development.

THIS IS A SURVEYOR'S SEAL

Not to be confused by seals, the magnificent, whiskered sea creatures. This seal is used by a surveyor. A surveyor is someone whose job it is to make a map of land. Land that someone FROM THE BANK is planning to turn into a SUB-DECISION!*

Why is this important? Glad you asked. Because I have discovered a plot by Jon (the dreaded hand-holder FROM THE BANK, heretoforever* referred to as "EVIL JON") to turn the Moody Mansion (the place where I live!) into a sub-decision!

CAUGHT YOU RED-HANDED, EVIL JON!

*sub-decision:
subdivision: an area of real estate composed of divided plots of land
Please remember this one, otherwise I will get carpal tunnel syndrome correcting it.

*heretoforever:
here to forever: from this point forward

Max Facts

34

And what happens to our little family if
EVIL JON tears down our house, you ask?
I believe the following scenarios are <u>self-explanationary</u>*.

I must devise a plan to foil him!

Max Fact

*self-explanationary:
self-explanatory:
no explanation needed

OPERATION EVIL JON

☐ FAILURE ☒ SUCCESS

I went to the bank to look for evidence (different than clues). I met a man named Mr. Middleton. He is my mom's boss. He has all these funny sayings, like: "Don't go looking for something unless you're ready to find nothing." I really don't know what he was talking about. When I go looking for something I always find what I'm looking for. But I digest*.

I went to EVIL JON'S desk...
AND GUESS WHAT I FOUND?!

There, in plain sight, was a paper
        with the COUNTY SURVEYOR SEAL on it!
I knew it!
I love it when I'm right! EVIL JON is planning to turn our new home into a sub-decision! But I have foiled the masterminded villain's plan!
I will present my evidence at dinner tonight.

HYPNOSIS—the art of hypnotizing someone into doing something that defries* common sense—such as clucking like a chicken when the doorbell rings, or barking like a dog when someone says "flibbersnibbets," or making my own mother believe that it was ME who got EVIL JON suspended from the bank for telling the bank people that Mom and EVIL JON were "involved in a relationship" (eww! yuck! gross!). So clearly, EVIL JON has hypnotized my mother. Shame.

P.S. As it turns out, the letter with the seal (non-aquatiatic*) was NOT for this property. However, what people often don't understand is that detective work is not an exactual* science.

Max Facts

* digest:
  digress: to wander from the main topic

* defries:
  defies: challenges the power of something or someone

* non-aquatiatic:
  nonaquatic: not living in the water

* exactual:
  exact: precise; correct. And yes, it is.

But the worst part.

The part that weighs so lowly on my heart is...

MAX DOES NOT BELIEVE I AM INNOCENT.

Can you believe it? My very own fiancé!*

CRASH. SHATTER.

That is the sound of Roxy Hunter's heart breaking.

Love cannot live without trust.

As a flower cannot live without sunlight,

or a bird cannot live without worms.

The box containing Estelle's things mocks me from the corner of my darkened room. Estelle and Ted's is a love from beyond the grave. Roxy and Max's is a love that is simply dead.

The engagement is off. I will inform him now.

Max Fact ➝

* I will never not believe Roxy again.
I will never not believe Roxy again.
I will never not believe Roxy again.
I will never not believe Roxy again.

(She made me write that 100 times—I'll spare you the other 96. You can thank me later.)

UNDEBELEEZADO*

Max Facts

*undebeleezado: unbelievable (I guess)

*momentoes: mementos: souvenirs

The case is back on!

Curious? Of course you are.

Then allow me to quench your curiosity.

When I gave Max the box of Estelle's momentoes*,

there was a paper in it.

That paper is called a DEED.

This kind of DEED is not:

   A) Helping an elderly woman to cross a street

Or:

   B) Feeding peanut brittle to homeless cats

It is:

   C) A piece of paper showing ownership of
      something—something like our house!

Someone desperately wants this deed to sell the
house to the sub-decision people! How brilliantly evil
is that?!

Max Fact

* extracute:
execute: to carry out;
to accomplish

Max suspects someone.
(Guess—go on—guess!!)
But he can't be certain unless he gets some
evidence in town tomorrow.
Max wants to catch the criminal in the act.
This is called, in the detective world, a

"STING."

(Not like what a bee does... but similar.)
In order to extracute* the sting we need
transportation. I remembered that
not-so-evil Jon got Ramma a job delivering
firewood. Ramma has a truck!
I will call him first thing tomorrow.

MY FIRST STING!

I am soooo excited!
Whatever will I wear?

HOW TO PLAN A STING

A STING is a kind of trap you lure a villain into.

YOU NEED...

A) BAIT: Just like in fishing. It is something juicy
    and tempting that you dangle in front of the
    villain. (For best results when baiting humans,
    don't use a worm.)

B) A TRAP: Once the archfiend goes for the bait,
    that is when you spring the trap.

C) CODE NAMES: DO NOT use your real name.
    It is for security reasons that are too complex
    to explain at this junctuation*.

Max Fact

*junctuation:
juncture: a point
in time that is
important because
several events occur
then

THE MORNING OF THE STING

Everything is in place
and ready to go.
Max—sorry—"Piglet" is in
town finding the necessary
dogumentation*.

REBECCA

Ramma—darn!—"Heffalump" is waiting
in the truck on the street.

And I, "Pooh," am inside,
watching "Woozle," our prey.
Can you guess who we suspect?
Come on.

It's REBECCA—
the estate lawyer/babysitter/repairwoman—

THIEF!!

Max Fact

* dogumentation:
documentation:
supporting
references

Max says that she has not been working
on the house but has been searching for
the precious deed ALL ALONG! He
doesn't think that she even works for
the Moody Estate lawyers.
I find the fiend is no friend!

Max Fact

* eludidated:
eluded: to evade or
escape by cunning or
daring

WOWZEREE! WHAT AN
UNBELIEVABLE DAY!!

Where do I start? I guess with...

THE STORY OF THE STING

Ramma and I followed Rebecca's
car to a retirement home.

Rebecca got out.

After some convincing, Ramma
waited in the truck while I
followed the Woozle in. I couldn't
find any clues. Until I saw...

The HAWK! And then I saw...

Rebecca dressed as a nurse! And
she had the DEED. She nearly
caught me, but I eludidated* her.
(Detectives need fast reflexes.)

When the coast was clear,
I went into the room. I saw an elderly lady.
I asked her if she was Rebecca's accomplish*.
She didn't know what I was talking about. I was
about to continue on with my investigationing* when
she told me that her name was... ESTELLE!!!!

ESTELLE MOODY

I asked her if she was Estelle
Moody. And she said she
hadn't heard that name in
years. But yes, she's Estelle
Moody!

Max Facts

She was NOT a ghost
from beyond! She was a
grandmother-type lady,
and very much alive!
Of course, that's when
Rebecca showed up again.

*accomplish:
accomplice: a person who helps
another in a crime

*investigationing:
investigating: to inquire
systematically; to search or
examine

*multifude:
multitude: many

THE SECRET ART OF DISGUISE

Disguise is an important part of a detective's life.
But beware! Disguises can be used
by criminal masterminds as well!

Here is the DASTARDLY Rebecca

in a multifude* of disguises.

This is NORMAL Rebecca.

Add an
eyepatch
+ hat =
PIRATE

Add a
space suit =
ASTRONAUT

Add a mustache

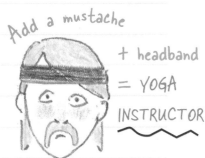

+ headband
= YOGA
INSTRUCTOR

Add sunglasses
+ helmet =
MOTORCYCLE
POLICEWOMAN

NYPD

Add a
nurse
outfit =

EVIL IMPOSTER NURSE!

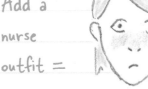

So Rebecca kidnapped us! She hurried me and Estelle Moody out of the retirement home and into her car. I hoped Ramma would see us, but alas...

 ★ HE WAS FAST ASLEEP IN THE TRUCK!

RULE ONE in any sting operation is...
        DON'T FALL ASLEEP!!

Then Rebecca drove us back to our home—ours meaning Estelle's used-to-be home, and my moved-in-so-peacefully-not-a-week-ago home—the Moody Mansion. We came in and there was Mom and the Not-So-Evil Jon (who, compared to Rebecca, seems about as evil as a box full of kittens, so I hereby decree that from this point forward he shall simply be known as "Jon"). And now the four of us were at the mercy of Evil Rebecca. Why? I'll tell you...

THE MAX FACTOR

So while we were on the Rebecca trail, this is what
was happening with Max (the poor dear).

Max went to the town hall to check some records,
and found the encriminalating* evidence, and took
it to the mayor, MR. MIDDLETON (my
mom's boss at the bank). Max
explained how Rebecca planned on
stealing the MOODY HOUSE
using a "ghost" corporation. Mr.
Middleton said he would take
Max to our sting. But instead,
he took him to the graveyard

that the hawk had led me to. Then he sealed
him in that stone tomb of death! The horror! The
horror! Then he told Max that they would hurt me
if Max tried to escape.

Max Fact

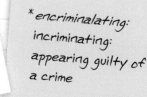

* encriminalating:
incriminating:
appearing guilty of
a crime

Max Facts

*monsterleum:
mausoleum: a magnificent
tomb

*pertrifried:
petrified: scared; terrified.
And, no, I wasn't really
that scared. Seriously. No.

What was Max to do?!
Naturally my beloved
and brave fiancé took
the path of COURAGE
and did not try to
escape. Defenseless, harmless,
bookwormy Max shut in that
dreaded monsterleum* with rats, and
spiders, and possibly VAMPIRES!
I can just see him shivering, shaking,
pertrifried* with fear!

spiders

Max in the
Middleton
Monsterleur

possible
vampires

rats

Meanwhile, back at MOODY MAYHEM...
Rebecca made us sit down for a nice Sunday
dinner—only it wasn't so nice. She told us if we
said anything when the developer got there
(more on him later), or tried to call the police, we
could say good-bye to little Maxie.

GASP!!

As it turns out, Rebecca (not her real name!
LIAR!) was selling the property not for the house,
but for the land—120 acres of it.
Apparently, the land is worth twelve million dollars.
I can't even imagine twelve million—my brain gets
bored with counting after 237.

(It was Jon who figured out about the land. You
know, maybe I wasn't 100 percent completely correct
about him—he kept his cool while we were hostages,
and he's pretty smart, and not a bad-looking fellow.)

When the developer was at the door, Rebecca said—
and remember this, oh faithful journal—

 "Anyone says anything out of line, and Max becomes a part of family history."

The man buying the stolen land's name was MR. FRANKLIN. He seemed to be a decent guy. I knew instantaniotiously* that he was not in league with Evil Rebecca. Then he gave her a check for more money than I knew existed in the world. And she gave him the DEED to the land.

It was that simple! Two pieces of paper get traded, and POOF! Rebecca sold the Moody Mansion, and it wasn't even hers to begin with! I couldn't let her get away with it. I had to do something.

BUT WHAT?!

Mom made me promise not to be a hero and jeopardize Max—but I couldn't just sit there and do nothing! So I did something—I invited Mr. Franklin to eat with us. After all, he looked like the kind of man who appreciates a good meal.

Max Facts

* instantaniotiously: instantaneously: right away

*brain brain: What Roxy is talking about is intuition. Intuition: quick and keen insight

I don't know why I did it. It was a feeling I had. And sometimes when you get that feeling in your stomach, you've just got to act on it. Everyone may tell you that you're wrong. Everyone may tell you what you SHOULD be doing. But that feeling in your stomach will never lie to you. It's like there is a brain in there that sometimes is smarter than your brain brain*.

And then I saw…
THE HAWK!
It was at the window!

I remembered Mr. Tibers
telling me that it was
a messenger from the spirit world. I had
originally thought it was Estelle, but she was
sitting right next to me—very much alive.
By process of elimitation* I realized that it
had to be… **TED!**

The hawk was sent by the ghost of
Theodore Caruthers! And there it was,
scratching at the window, trying to convey a
message to me! But what was it? Time was
of the insense*!

Max Facts

*elimitation:
We've done this one
already, I believe.

*insense:
essence: absolutely critical

And then Rebecca said something.
And it was like finding the piece of a
jigsaw puzzle that makes everything
fall into place.

Rebecca said,
"Don't go looking for
something unless you're ready
to find trouble."
This sounded a LOT like...

Mr. Middleton

What Mom's boss (and mayor)
said, which was, "Don't go
looking for something unless
you're ready to find nothing."
And his name was...

And I knew I'd seen that
name before.

BUT WHERE?!

Max Facts

* geniusity: genius

* monsterleum: we've done this one

* accomplish: this one, too

And then, in a flash of geniusity*, I remembered where!

The Middleton Monsterleum*! And Rebecca had said that Max was "in a cold scary place," and was "going to be part of family history."

FAMILY HISTORY.

And guess who Max had gone to see that morning...

MR. MIDDLETON!

He was Rebecca's accomplish* and dad! And he was holding Max hostage in the Middleton tomb of doom! And that is how I put the puzzle together.

So, in one fell swap*, I solved the mystery of the criminal's identity and discovered Max's location! Just then, the POLICE ARRIVED! (Yay, Ramma! He woke up just in time and called the cops.) Rebecca tried to make a break for it—and then I realized (sometimes these rebelations* come to you in a flash) that TED was the ghost! Ted had tried to warn us about Rebecca the very first time we met her, by making a huge chunk of the ceiling fall! Well, if he could do it once, he could do it again. So right when Rebecca was standing under the spot, I called out to Ted—and guess what??

THE PLASTER FELL RIGHT ON REBECCA!!!

We did it! We caught the villain! Gosh, we're good.

← Max Facts

*in one fell swap: in one fell swoop: all at once

*rebelations: revelations: an uncovering; a bringing to light

Well, well, well.

Once again, I, Roxy Hunter, super-sleuth, have proven crime does not pay. Or at least not while I'm on the case.

ROBERTA (not Rebecca) Middleton is the bad seed daughter of the bad apple Mr. Middleton. He had discovered the HUGE extent of the Moody land. Not even Estelle knew it! And because he was the mayor and the head of the bank, he could sneakify* the deals and no one would know—not even bank assistant Jon! And of course, I was right about Max's location. He WAS in the tomb.

← Max Facts

*In summimnation:
in summation: a statement reviewing points and conclusions

*sneakify:
sneak and falsify: Roxy means
falsify: to knowingly report untrue information

HOW GHOSTS MOVE THINGS

ceiling chunk

spectra-pushulation applied

ghost

It falls on Evil Rebecca

A ghost moves things using paranormal spectra-pushulation*. Ghosts are disembothered* spirits. They have no bodies. But because they are energy (a weird form of energy that Max says doesn't scientifically exist—riiiight. Like that chunk of plaster fell by coincidence*) a ghost can throw its energy at an object and force it to move... And that is paranormal spectra-pushulation!

Although it would still be really hard for a ghost to tie its shoelaces, or clean its room.

Max Facts

*spectra-pushulation: Don't ask me.

*disembothered:
disembodied: freed (the soul or spirit) from the body

*the plaster fell by coincidence: It fell because of gravity. That's all.

THE TRAGIC AND TRUE TALE OF TED AND ESTELLE

I remember reading that the Greek god of love was blind and he would just shoot these love arrows all over the place. And if you got hit by one, then you'd just fall in love blindly. And while I believe that blind people can do many brilliant things (Ray Charles, for example) I still wouldn't trust them with a bow and arrow.

Such as it was with Ted and Estelle. They fell blindly, truly in love, and wanted to be together forever. But Estelle's dad didn't want them to marry. Estelle's family was rich, and Ted's was poor. (As if that makes a difference!) It was the year 1944. World War II was raging. And Ted came to the house to ask for Estelle's hand in marriage before being "shipped out." (I believe that means being put on a ship and being sent out to war.)

He arrived that night in his uniform.
said he looked so handsome that she
her father would let them marry.
alas, no. Her father threatened
with a shotgun! Ted refused to
leave, knowing LOVE CONCKERS*
ALL! But the gun went off and
BLASTED a hole in the ceiling—
YES, the same hole that came down
on Rebecca/Roberta's head a bazillion
years later! Estelle's father swore it
was an accident. But Ted, noble Ted,

TED

ESTELLE'S DAD

knew that this was not how he wanted to take Estelle
away (covered in plaster dust). He swore he would come
back for Estelle. Three days later, his ship was sunk by
a tropeedo* and Ted died. I guess his ghost came back
and has been waiting for her ever since.

Max Facts

* conckers:
conquers: look it up

* tropeedo:
torpedo: I'll give you this
one. It is a cigar-shaped
explosive shot from
submarines.

Estelle's story was so sad it touched us all, especially sweet Ramma who was moved to tears. But then, Estelle said something so simple and so profunded*. She said that life went on. And she was glad it did. And I guess I know what she means. I never thought me and Mom would recover when my dad died. But we did—little by little. It's like when you go camping and you see an area that has been destroyed by a forest fire. It is all black and dead. But when you come back the next summer a little green has begun to grow. And when you come back the following summer, green is everywhere. I guess—if you give anything time, it heals. That is my new theory— "healiotimeosity*." FLIBBERSNIBBETS! I just realized I have Estelle's engagement ring— I will give it to her at once.

Max Facts

*profunded:
profound: penetrating beyond what is superficial or obvious

*healiotimeosity: What Roxy means here is that "time heals all wounds." And that Mrs. Hunter has healed enough after the death of Mr. Hunter to start dating again, which is quite mature of Roxy to notice, actually.

WOWZEREE!

I just gave Estelle her ring back.

She is staying in her old room tonight (was mine), and I asked her if we would have to move now that she was back. And she smiled in this nice warm grandmatastic* way, and said no, she had already taken steps to make sure we could stay at the MOODY MANSION as long as we liked. I don't know what those steps are, but if she taught them to me, I'd be happy to dance them for a couple of years.

(And Max, before you go correcting me—I know the difference between "taking steps" and "dance steps" thankyouverymuch.)

So we get to live in this fantabulous house!

*grandmatastic:
fantastically
grandmotherly

Max Fact

It's a good thing I am writing right now, because I am speechless. You won't believe what I just saw.

I'm sleeping on the couch ('cause Estelle is in my room—remember?). And I woke up suddenly. I don't know why. I just did. And I looked up and saw something... It was Ted and Estelle!! I pinched myself to make sure I wasn't dreaming. And I wasn't, I tell you!! Estelle was young again (like in the photo) and in her wedding dress! **AND THEY WERE GHOSTS!**

I, Roxy Hunter, being of sound mind and body, SAW GHOSTS! And the most amazingest thing happened... They kissed. A kiss that has waited a kajillion years. And then, just like that, they disappeared—because their love had been re-unificated* from beyond the grave.

It was the most beautiful thing I have ever seen.
And that is the way we closed the

Mystery of the Moody Ghost.

Undebeleezado.

The funniest thing I have
learned through this roller—
ghoster adventure is that...
It is not bricks, wood,
windows, or a beautiful
fireplace that make a home.
It is something else.
It is the people who are in
it, and what they feel in
their hearts for one another.
That's what makes a home.

*re-unificated:
reunited: to unify
again. This is the last
one. You're on your
own now.

Max Fact

R. H. out.

Serenity Falls:
A Staying Poem

You don't have galleries and
museums that inspire me.
You don't have high-rises as far
as the eye can see.
But you have history and ghosts
and beauty I must say,
So here in Serenity Falls
I think

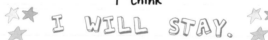 I WILL STAY.

I ♥ SERENITY FALLS